W9-BHP-586

Written by Walter Wangerin Jr.

PETER'S FIRST EASTER

Illustrated by Timothy Ladwig

Zonder**kidz**

The Children's Group of ZondervanPublishingHouse

Library of Congress Cataloging-in-Publication Data

Wangerin, Walter.

Peter's First Easter / written by Walter Wangerin Jr. : illustrated by Timothy Ladwig.

    p.   cm.

*Summary: The story of the last days in Jesus' life, from the Last Supper to his crucifixion
and resurrection, told from the point of view of one of his disciples, Simon Peter.*

ISBN 0-310-22217-6 (hardcover : alk. paper)

*1. Peter, the Apostle, Saint — Juvenile literature.   2. Jesus Christ — Biography — Passion
Week — Juvenile literature.   3. Jesus Christ — Resurrection — Juvenile literature. [1. Jesus
Christ — Passion. 2. Jesus Christ — Resurrection. 3. Peter, the Apostle, Saint. 4. Easter.]
I. Ladwig, Tim, ill. II. Title.*

BS2515.W35   2000

232.96 — DC21   *99-11590*

                    CIP

                    AC

*This edition printed on acid-free paper and meets the American National Standards Institute
Z39.48 standard.*

*Published in association with the literary agency of Alive Communications, Inc.,
1465 Kelly Johnson Blvd. #320, Colorado Springs, CO 80920.*

Printed in China

00 01 02 03 04 05 06/❖ HK/ 10 9 8 7 6 5 4 3 2 1

Aaron, Caleb, Elizabeth: Rejoice in that fish after Easter! — W.W.

For David — T.L.

1

The Last Supper

Jesus was sad when we climbed the stairs.

He was sad when we entered the upper room and took our places around the table. He was sad when we started to eat.

But I didn't notice how sad he was until he opened his mouth and spoke those terrible, terrible words.

It was Thursday evening, one hour after sunset. The windows and doors were locked. Lamp flames sent shadows into all the corners of the room. Outside in the night, there were people looking to arrest Jesus; but inside we were safe. We were like his family, you know: his disciples, his closest friends. Jesus was our Lord and teacher, and we loved him.

Well, but in those days I figured I loved him the most because he had given me a special name. I am Simon the son of John, but Jesus called me *Peter*, which means "rock." He said I was like a big stone, the kind you could build a building on. Oh, I loved him so much that sometimes it made me laugh out loud.

I also love to eat. That's what I was doing Thursday evening, and that's why I didn't notice Jesus' sadness. I was eating roasted lamb and bread as thin as crackers. I was eating some leaves so bitter they made my nose run—but I dipped them in a fruit sauce to take the bitterness away.

I was chewing and chewing and swallowing when suddenly Jesus said: "One of you is going to betray me."

I stopped eating and saw that there were tears in Jesus' eyes. He was so sad! And these are the terrible words: "This very night," he said, "one of you will lead my enemies to me, and they will tie me up, and then they will kill me."

What! *Kill Jesus?*

All of us sat still and stared. Some of us said, "Is it me, Jesus? Is it me?" Only one of us kept eating.

John sat between me and Jesus, so I nudged him and nodded toward the Lord. John knew what I meant. He leaned upon Jesus and whispered, "Who, Lord? Who could do such a thing?"

Slowly, Jesus took some bitter leaves and reached to a dish of fruit sauce. Judas Iscariot—the only disciple still eating—was dipping his own leaves in that dish.

Jesus said, "The one who is dipping with me, he will betray me."

Judas dropped the leaves and snatched his hand away. He bared his teeth in a grin. "Me, Lord?" he said. "You don't mean *me!*"

Jesus said, "What you have to do—go, do it quickly."

Right away Judas got up. He tried to say something, but instead he opened the door and went out into the night.

No one moved. Chilly breezes caused the lamp flames to flicker. Shadows troubled Jesus' face. I jumped up and slammed the door.

Jesus ate nothing that night, yet he commanded us to eat *and* to drink. He took some bread and blessed it and broke it and gave it to us, saying, "Take this. Eat it." We did. But while we were chewing the bread, he said, "This is my body."

His body? *Oh, Lord, how could I swallow your body?*

Next he took a cup of wine and thanked God and said, "Drink this, all of you." We obeyed him. But again, while we were taking little sips, he said, "This is my blood, poured out for the forgiveness of sins."

Body and *blood*, now! Who could ever forget such a meal? My heart was hammering inside my chest. Surely, this would be a night like no other night in all the world.

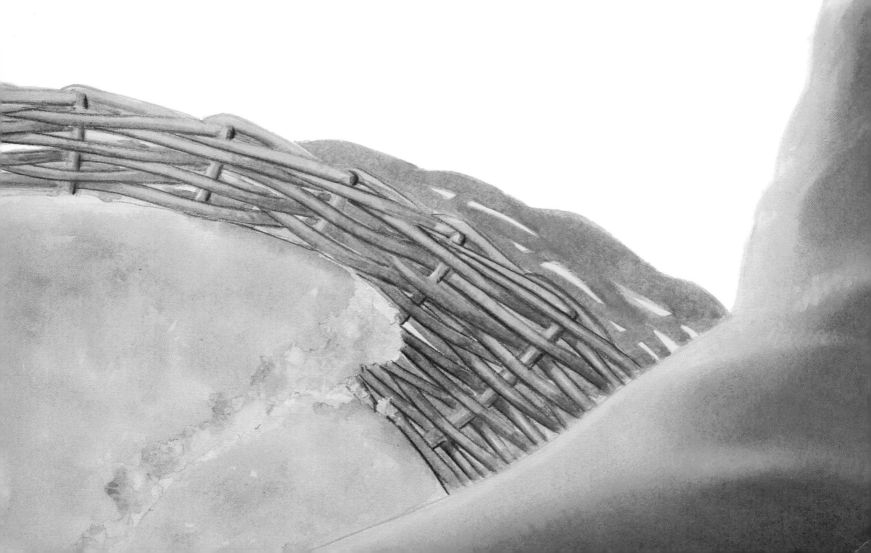

Leaving Jerusalem

An hour later we were all walking down
the dark streets of Jerusalem.

For as long as ten minutes Jesus prayed out loud. "Father," he
said, "keep my friends safe from the Evil One."

When he was done praying, he walked on in silence, thinking,
thinking.

We went through a city gate and crossed the Kidron Valley, then
we began to climb a path up the Mount of Olives.

Suddenly Jesus said, "You are all going to run away from me
tonight."

Sometimes my feelings are so strong that I talk before I think, so
I shouted, "Not me! Not me, Lord! Everyone else might run away
from you, but not me!"

Jesus came and put his hand on my shoulder and looked at me with his sad eyes. "Peter, Peter," he said, "you will do worse than run away. Before the rooster crows tomorrow morning, you will deny me three times."

"No!" I said. "No, no, no! Even if I have to die, I will never deny you."

On the Mount of Olives

When we reached the top of the Mount,

Jesus told the disciples to wait in the clearing while he prayed. Then he took John and James and me with him into the Garden of Gethsemane.

What was that noise? It sounded like wind in dead trees. What was it?

It was Jesus! He was groaning while he walked: "Ohhh, ohhh."

Finally he stopped and told us to sit down, but he kept standing. Under a thousand stars I could see sweat on his forehead, sweat as thick as blood.

"Oh, my friends," he groaned, "I am scared to death. Please keep watch with me." Then he walked off into the trees.

At first there was silence. Then there was a heavy thump on the ground and groaning. Jesus had fallen down. I almost got up to run to him—but then I heard his voice, and I left him alone. He was crying, *Daddy! Daddy!* Jesus was sobbing like a little boy: *O Father, take this cup of suffering away from me!*

Over and over, softer and softer he said these words, like singing. I began to feel woozy in my head. He said, *But you, my God—let your will be done, not mine—*

That's the last I heard. I cuddled against John's back, and listened to the breezes, and drifted, drifted....

The next thing I knew, Jesus was standing over us, saying, "Get up! My betrayer is coming." He turned and walked out of the garden.

My whole body was tingling. The air was full of dreamy noises, metal-clankings, feet-marchings. What was happening?

Oh, no! I had been sleeping!

I jumped up and ran after Jesus, and right away I saw the soldiers coming up the mount with torches and swords, and here were the disciples all huddled together—and in the middle stood Judas Iscariot, grinning.

As soon as he recognized Jesus, he raised his hand and hollered, "Hello, Master!"

The idiot, yelling as if they were miles apart!

Now he crept toward Jesus, grinning and blinking and crouching down like a dog. When he was face to face with Jesus, Judas Iscariot went up on his toes and said, "My dear teacher," and kissed him!

One of the soldiers shouted, "Is that the man, then?" Judas stepped aside. The soldier came forward with a rope, and I went crazy with rage.

I pulled out my sword and ran at the soldier and slashed his ear clean off his head. A bad swing. This time I took a deadly aim, but before I could attack someone grabbed me from behind, someone very strong.

He stripped the sword from my hand and yanked my arms back. "Everyone who takes the sword," he hissed, "shall die by the sword."

It was Jesus! All my bones went as soft as soup. I said, "I'm only trying to help," but Jesus moved past me and picked up the ear that I had cut off and touched it to the side of the soldier's head and healed it.

Now, this is how bad the world was that night: the soldier whom Jesus had healed seized him and tied him tightly with the rope. And the disciples whom Jesus loved—they all ran away.

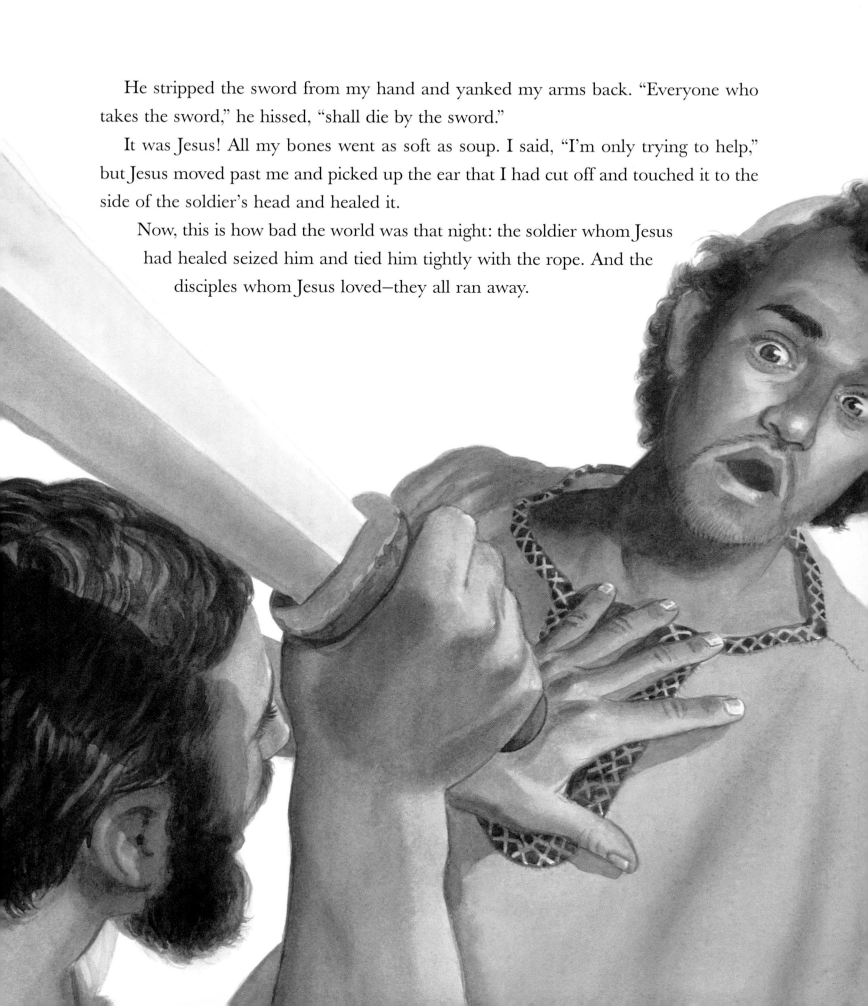

4

In the Courtyard of the High Priest

Me, I didn't exactly run away from Jesus.

I followed him. Secretly. I snuck down dark alleys, keeping up with the tramp of the soldiers' feet.

It was long past midnight. The stars were gone. A cold wind blew through Jerusalem. The city was dark and sleeping—all but the house of the High Priest, where people were gathering with noise and torch-light.

It was to that house, high on Zion, that the soldiers led my dear Lord Jesus. When they arrived, the iron gate swung open and they all marched into the courtyard.

Just as the gate was closing I saw John slip inside.

"John!" I called, running up to the bars. "Let me in!"

He heard me, but he pretended he didn't.

"John! It's me, Peter!"

He motioned for me to shut up, then moved to a young maid and murmured something behind her ear. She glanced my way. When she turned to see who had spoken to her, John had vanished.

Frowning, then, and staring hard at my face, the maid came to the gate and opened it. I walked in as if I belonged there, but she kept staring. There were soldiers everywhere in the courtyard. They all had knives and swords. So I pulled my cloak up over my nose and crouched down by a fire.

That girl was like a mosquito. She circled closer and closer. All at once she clapped her hands and exclaimed, "Yes, I *do* know you! You're a friend of the prisoner."

She poked a soldier and pointed to the window of a room. We could see Jesus standing. "This man," she said, meaning me, "is with that man in there."

When the soldier started staring at me, I growled like a lion: "I don't know what she's talking about." Then I got up and stalked across the courtyard to the window where Jesus was.

It didn't take me long to realize that horrible things were happening in that room. People were screaming, "He's guilty! He's guilty! He said he'd destroy the Temple itself!"

I saw the High Priest raise an oil lamp to Jesus' face and say, "I command you to tell the truth, the whole truth, and nothing but the truth: are you the Christ, the Son of God?"

The room fell silent.

Jesus, gazing directly into the High Priest's eyes, said: "I am."

"Blasphemy!" cried the High Priest as if someone had slapped him. He smashed the lamp and began to rip his clothes. "Jesus of Nazareth has sinned against the most high God!" he cried. "What is your verdict? What shall we do with this man?"

"Kill him! Kill him!" the people yelled. They hit Jesus, they spit on him, and they yelled: "Put him to *death!*"

How could I watch that and do nothing? I was trying to figure out what to do, when suddenly someone touched my arm. I jumped straight up and whirled around and found three soldiers and a servant all glaring at me. The one who touched me said, "The maid was right. You *are* one of his followers."

"Not me!" I shouted. "I swear to you, I'm not."

But the servant grabbed my sleeve and said, "Liar! I saw you. The man whose ear you cut off—that man is my cousin."

This was more than I could take. I cursed and swore and roared: "I have never even *met* the man named Jesus!"

With all my might, I tore my sleeve from the servant and spun around—and there in the window was Jesus, staring back at me, his eyes so sad, his eyes so very sad.

And then the rooster started to crow.

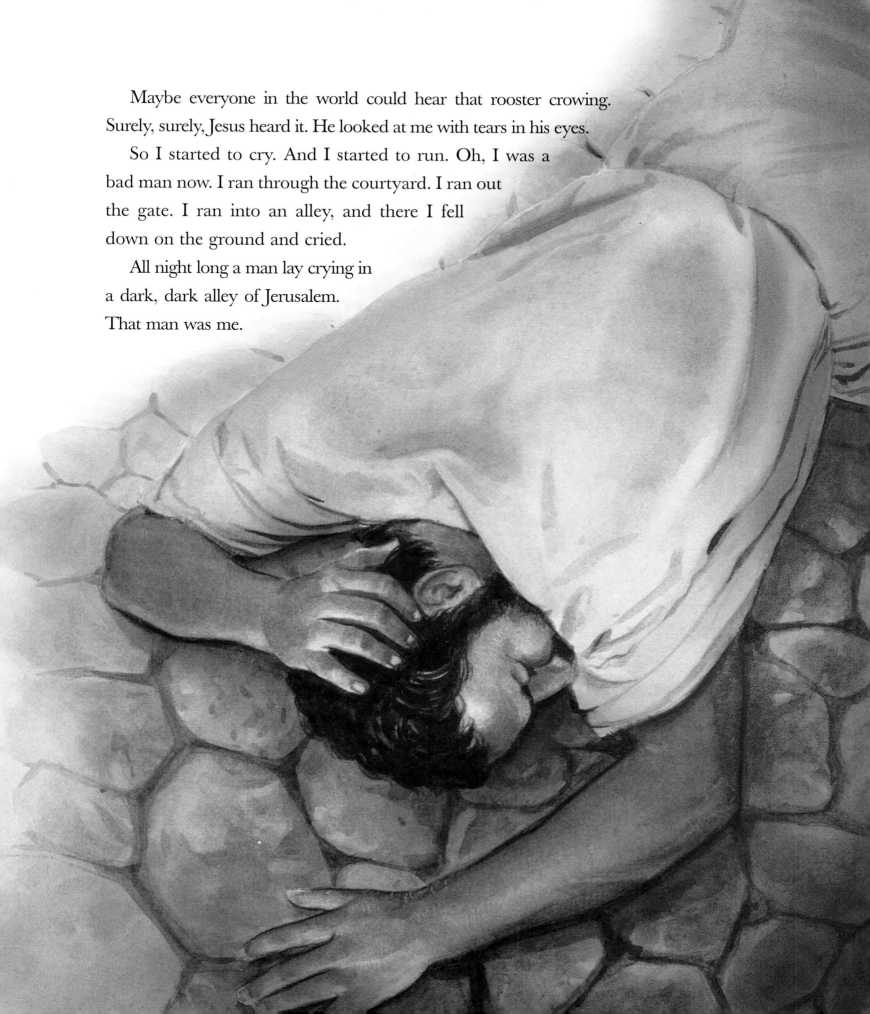

Maybe everyone in the world could hear that rooster crowing. Surely, surely, Jesus heard it. He looked at me with tears in his eyes.

So I started to cry. And I started to run. Oh, I was a bad man now. I ran through the courtyard. I ran out the gate. I ran into an alley, and there I fell down on the ground and cried.

All night long a man lay crying in a dark, dark alley of Jerusalem. That man was me.

5

Hiding

I was such a bad man now, that I didn't
deserve for people to like me. They shouldn't even *look* at me. So
at dawn on Friday I went into hiding.

But let me tell you something: I still loved Jesus. Do you
understand this? I wanted to be close to him. So wherever the
soldiers took him, I followed, sneaking from hiding place to hiding
place like a rabbit. Like a robber.

Like the ugliest person in all the world.

The ugliest—yes! A year ago Jesus had called me by the ugliest
name there is. At the time I thought he was wrong, but now I
guessed he was probably right.

He had been teaching us the grand plan of his life: that he would
go to Jerusalem, that he would suffer many things, and that he
would be killed. Killed! Well, from the moment I heard that plan, I
hated it, and I told him so.

He was still teaching. *And after three days,* he was saying, *I will rise again*—but I wasn't listening. I walked straight up to him and said, "God forbid that this should ever happen to you."

Jesus snapped his mouth shut. His eyes made sparks of fire, and he said, *Get behind me, Satan. If you hate this plan, you hate the ways of God. I came to give my life away for the lives of many people.*

"Satan." Jesus had called me by the ugly name of "Satan." How could I let anyone look at me if he was right? That's why I hid myself all Friday long.

But I never stopped loving Jesus. And that is why, wherever they took him, I followed.

6

At the Governor's Palace

Friday morning was grey and cold and wet.

Even before the city woke up, the Priests and soldiers led Jesus to the palace of the Roman Governor.

"Pontius Pilate!" the High Priest cried. "Come out and judge this man, this Jesus of Nazareth. He is guilty of crimes deserving death."

The Governor came out with a sneer on his face. He didn't like us Jews very much. He sat down in a big chair and said, "It's raining. Hurry up and tell me why you think he should die."

"For one," the High Priest said, "he tells people not to

pay taxes to the Emperor. For another, he says that he is a king, Christ the King!"

Pontius Pilate leaned forward to take the measure of this criminal. He gazed at a thin man with steadfast eyes and raindrops on his hair. The man was shivering in the cold. His face was bruised. The ropes cut into his skin. But he looked back at the Roman with no rage nor hate—just patience and a perfect knowing.

Pilate said, "Are you the king of the Jews?"

Jesus said, "You say so."

Pilate squinted more closely at Jesus, then he sat back and waved his hand to shoo the priests and the soldiers away.

"Go home," he said. "I don't find any fault in the man."

The Chief Priest climbed halfway up the Governor's steps and said, "Look harder, sir! He stirs up the citizens! He causes riots against your government!"

More and more people were gathering now. The High Priest turned to them and cried: "You know the evil of Jesus, don't you?"

"He's a sly one!" the people shouted.

"Disloyal!"

"Right! He breaks the laws of Moses and of Rome."

"You see?" the High Priest said to Pilate. "He's a rebel, a dangerous man!"

Pilate said to Jesus, "How do you answer these charges?"

Jesus stayed silent.

Pilate said, "Have you nothing to say for yourself?"

Nothing. Jesus stood like a white column, calm and kind.

"Okay, okay," he said to the Chief Priest and the crowds, "I know what I'm going to do. I will release one prisoner, and I'll let you choose which one. Should I release the murderer named Barabbas? Or shall I release Jesus, the king of the Jews."

It was a trick, and I liked it! Barabbas was wicked. He truly belonged in jail. Surely no one would want him free in the streets. They *had* to pick Jesus.

Pontius Pilate stood up to address the entire crowd. It was amazing how many people had come out in the drizzling rain. "Which man," he called out, "do you choose?"

Immediately the people shouted, "Give us Barabbas!"

Pilate was shocked. "Then what should I do with Jesus of Nazareth?" he cried.

Louder than ever the huge crowd thundered, "CRUCIFY HIM!"

"Why? Why? What evil has he done?"

The High Priest now stood equal to Pilate. "By our law he ought to die, because he called himself the Son of God."

Pilate cried, "Your laws are not my laws. Deal with him yourselves."

Then the High Priest delivered his final threat: "If you release this man, you are not a friend of Caesar. Anyone who makes himself king is an enemy of the *real* king, Caesar!"

Pontius Pilate looked scared. A thousand people were ready to riot, screaming, "CRUCIFY HIM! CRUCIFY HIM!"

So the Roman Governor sat down and shrugged his shoulders.

He released the evil Barabbas.

Jesus he ordered to be whipped and then to be crucified.

7

On Golgotha

What did I see that Friday? What sorrowful things did I witness?

I saw my Lord Jesus bowed and bloody, trying to carry a heavy beam of wood. Criminals are supposed to carry part of their crosses out to the place of their dying. But Jesus kept falling down. So the soldiers commanded another man to carry the beam to a little hill called Golgotha.

And what did I see? I saw the soldiers lay Jesus down on the ground. They stretched his arms to the ends of the beam, then pounded spikes through his bones into the wood.

I saw them lift the whole beam up with Jesus hanging from it, up to the top of a very strong pole. They put a sign there that said: JESUS, THE KING OF THE JEWS. Then they came down and spiked his ankles to the pole.

It was misty cold. The wind was blowing. All of Jesus' ribs were showing through his skin like a skeleton—but I heard him say this holy thing.

He looked up, then he looked down at the people around him. "Father, forgive them," he said. "They don't know what they are doing."

It was so holy that I could hardly breathe.

But the people were laughing! They were pointing at him and sneering: "He saved others, but he can't save his own *self!*"

There were two thieves crucified with Jesus, one on his right and one on his left.

The man on his left was laughing like everyone else! "Hey, you Christ!" he cried. "Save yourself, and save me too!"

But the man on his right said, "What's the matter with you? You and I deserve to die, but this man didn't do anything wrong!" Then he lowered his voice and whispered, "Jesus? Jesus, please remember me when you come into your kingdom."

Jesus looked at that thief a while. "I promise you," he whispered back, "today you will be with me in Paradise."

I, Simon Peter, hiding from everyone and from everything–I wished that Jesus were speaking to me.

Now the clouds grew thicker and darker. A true rain started to fall. People ran back into the city until the only ones left on the wet hill were the soldiers, a few women, and just one man.

No, that man wasn't me. It was John.

Among the women were Mary Magdalene and Mary the mother of Jesus.

"Woman," he said to his mother. She was crying so hard that John had to hold her up. "Woman," Jesus said, "let the man beside you be your son." And to John he said, "She is your mother."

Hugging her tightly, John led Mary away from such sadness, and then almost no one was left on Golgotha.

Now the clouds in the heavens shut down like a door, and the world became as black as night, and out of the darkness came a loud voice, wailing, "My God! My God!" It was Jesus. I could not see, but I could hear his cry rise up to the sky: "My God, why have you *forsaken* me?"

No one answered. No one answered him. I covered my face and did not move for an hour, for two hours.

Then I heard my dear Lord murmur two soft words. He said, "I'm thirsty."

So I crept out of my hiding place and I took a sponge and filled it with vinegar and stuck it on a stick and reached it up to Jesus' mouth, and he drank.

He drank. Did he know it was I? Did he know I was there?

When he was done drinking, Jesus sighed, "It is finished."

Then he said a little prayer, the one that children pray before they go to sleep. "Father," he said, "into your hands I place my spirit."

What did I see that Friday? And what did I witness?

I saw the head of Jesus sink down between his shoulders. I saw his body sag. I heard a long, long breath go out of his mouth, and I waited. I waited. But I never heard another breath go into him again.

Jesus was dead.

8

In the Tomb

They buried him.

On the Friday of my hiding, just before the sun went down, a man named Joseph came and lowered the body of Jesus from the cross. He wrapped it in a long white linen cloth and carried it into his own tomb, a grave carved in solid stone.

Joseph rolled a flat stone like a wheel against the door to the tomb, and then he went away.

Alone, then, I went to that flat stone and touched it. I touched my name. Peter. The rock.

But what good is a stone when no one can build a building on it? What good is the stone that can only shut in a dead man?

O Peter, what is to become of you now?

9

Sunday Morning

For me, Saturday was a dead and dreadful day.

One by one all the disciples snuck back to the upper room where we had eaten with Jesus on Thursday—all but Judas. We locked the door and blew out the candles so no one could tell we were there. We were scared.

We had hoped that Jesus was the Redeemer of Israel, but he had died. All our hopes had died too.

We didn't eat. We didn't talk. We sat in sadness and in darkness, all alone.

Then someone started to bang on the door. I thought the soldiers had come, until the person hollered, "Peter! Peter!" It was a woman's voice.

"Go away," I shouted.

"Peter! Open the door. It's me, Mary Magdalene!"

I cracked the door. Light burst into the room. Why, it was Sunday morning! But I said, "Hush, woman! The soldiers will hear you."

"Oh, Peter, you donkey!" Mary laughed. She was with James' mother and Joanna and Salome. They were all laughing.

"The angels," they cried, "have sent us with messages! Oh, Peter, come out! Come, see what we have seen!"

Mary pulled me down the steps and made me run through the city with her.

"We went to the tomb," she said, "to rub oils on Jesus' body. But when we got there, the stone was rolled away, and the tomb was empty, Peter, and we were so scared. But there was an angel, and he told us not to be afraid, and he said,

"You're looking for Jesus, but he isn't here. He is risen, just as he promised."

Mary burst out laughing again and ran ahead of me all the way to the tomb.

"Look inside," she said.

I did. I saw the linen cloth lying by itself, but nothing else. No *body* was here, either living or dead. So what was I supposed to think? I stood up, more scared than ever.

Mary said, "Peter, don't you remember his promise?—that he would rise again on the third day?"

I pushed her out of my way and ran as fast as I could to the upper room again. I slammed the door and locked it. Mary was a fool, and I was scared, because if our enemies would steal the body of Jesus, they would surely kill us too.

When the evening came, Thomas said that at least we ought to eat something, so he went out to find some food, while we argued about whether to light a lamp at all.

All at once Jesus was in the room with us!

He frightened us. We all backed away.

He said, "Peace be with you," and that made things worse. This was a ghost that could talk!

But then he did three things: He opened his hands and showed us the scars from the spikes; he sang the beautiful words again, almost as if they were a lullaby, *Peace be with you*; and he smiled at us. He smiled like in the olden days, but he smiled in a new way too, like the morning sun at the beginning of the world.

John started to giggle. James swatted his leg and laughed out loud. Soon all the disciples were laughing till the tears ran down their cheeks, so glad were they to see the Lord. Yes, it *was* the third day! Yes, he *had* arisen from the dead.

He said, "Just as the Father sent me into the world, so I am sending you. Go out and do my work." Then he came near and breathed on each one of us and said, "Receive the Holy Spirit. The sins you forgive, they are forgiven."

Well, not *all* the disciples laughed. For one, Thomas wasn't even there. And when the others told him what had happened, he wouldn't believe them until Jesus came back again, one week later, and proved to Thomas that he was really and truly alive.

And for another—me. I could not laugh with the others, because I didn't know what Jesus thought of me now. I was the one, you see, who had sworn that he had never even met Jesus. I was so afraid for my own life that I denied him three times.

I was so glad that he was alive again. And I never stopped loving him. But I didn't laugh. I hid behind James and John.

10

Fishing and Forgiveness

Here, now, is the last part and the best part of my story.

After we saw Jesus in the upper room, many of us traveled back to Galilee, where we used to live. Then just yesterday afternoon, I said that I was going fishing. It's the job we used to do before Jesus came to us and said, "Follow me," and we became his disciples.

So James, John, Thomas, and four more men went with me to the seashore. In the evening we sailed out on the water and began to cast our nets. It wasn't a good trip. We spent the whole night casting but by early this morning we had caught exactly nothing.

Then someone called from shore: "Children, do you have something to eat?"

"No," I shouted back, yanking my nets in for the last time.

"Tell you what," the man called. "Cast your nets on the right side of the boat and see what happens."

"Right side, left side, what's the difference," I grumbled. Who did that amateur think he was? We did this for a living.

But John—who is forever cheerful these days—called out, "Okay!" and obeyed the stranger.

Well, as soon as John's net hit water, so many fish jumped in that it began to drag the whole boat down!

"Peter!" John's eyes were sparkling. "Don't you know who that is?"

"Who?"

"It's the Lord!"

Sometimes my feelings are so strong that I act before I think. *The Lord?* I jumped in the water and swam to shore.

Yes! It *was* the Lord. And he had a fire burning. He said, "Help them bring the fish in, and let's eat."

I did. In that single catch this morning we landed a hundred and fifty-three fish. A happy day.

We took several of the best fish and cleaned them and broiled them and then lay down in the grass to eat them.

This time my eating did not keep me from noticing Jesus' face. I think I took maybe one bite before I saw that he was not eating—just like the last time. But the difference was, he was staring straight at me. At me and no one else.

Oh, my face burned like a fire then, and the fish stuck in my throat. I could not chew. I could not swallow. I hung my head, scarcely breathing.

After a while Jesus said, "Simon, son of John, do you love me more than these?"

He didn't call me by my special name. I didn't look up at him. I whispered, "Yes, Lord. You know that I love you."

He said, "Feed my lambs."

He didn't say anything for almost a minute, but he kept looking at me, and I kept looking down at the ground.

Jesus said, "Simon, son of John, do you love me?"

I whispered, "Yes, Lord, you know that I love you."

He said, "Tend my sheep."

No one was eating now. I was shaking. When Jesus spoke again, the tears spilled down from my eyes.

"Simon, son of John," he said, "do you love me?"

Three times. It was the same number of times that I had denied him. That's why I was crying now. "Lord, you know all things," I said so softly that maybe he couldn't hear me. "You *know* I love you."

Well, when I had said that, Jesus leaned over and put his arms around me and hugged me so tight that I burst into big boo-hoos, crying like a little baby, crying for happiness, for sheer pure happiness.

He lifted me up and put me on my feet. He gazed into my eyes, and he gave me a job to do for him for the rest of my life.

Jesus said, "Feed my sheep."

That's what happened just this morning! And I have run as fast as I can to tell you the good news.

Jesus has forgiven me. Three times I hurt him, and he took the hurt, and he went down to death with it. When he rose from the dead, the hurt was gone. And when I was so sorry for what I did, he came and loved me three times back again—and now I have so much of his love that I can love you just like Jesus! Forgiveness! We are both forgiven!

How do I know? Well, when we were done eating Jesus smiled and said the very same thing he said when first he called me. *Peter*, he said—Peter, you know, his big stone! *Peter*, he said, *follow me*.

Sometimes my feelings are so strong that I talk before I think. "Yes!" I cried. "Oh, Jesus, I will follow you forever!"